A LIFT-THE-FLAP STORY
SCOOTER'S CHRISTMAS
Harriet Ziefert • Pictures by Rick Brown

HarperFestival
A Division of HarperCollinsPublishers

There were presents hidden in his house.
Scooter knew it and he wanted to find them.

"Where are my presents?" Scooter asked. Scooter's daddy answered, "You'll have to wait until Christmas morning for them."

"Where are my presents?" Scooter asked.
"I'm not telling," answered Scooter's mommy.

Scooter looked all over for his presents.
He looked high…

and he looked low.

He looked downstairs.

And he looked upstairs.

Scooter looked under the pillows.

He looked under the bed.

Scooter's mommy said, "I know it's hard to wait, but Santa will bring your presents soon."

Then came Christmas morning.

And there were presents. Lots of them.

Merry Christmas, Mommy!
Merry Christmas, Daddy!